The Jungle House

and

The Snake Who Came To Stay

Two Short Stories

by

Julia Donaldson

Illustrated by Philippe Dupasquier

You do not need to read this page –
just get on with the book!

First published in 2005 in Great Britain by
Barrington Stoke Ltd
18 Walker Street, Edinburgh, EH3 7LP

www.barringtonstoke.co.uk

Reprinted 2008

ISBN: 978-1-84299-333-0

Printed in Great Britain by Bell & Bain Ltd

MEET THE AUTHOR – JULIA DONALDSON

What is your favourite animal?

A cat

What is your favourite boy's name?

Hamish

What is your favourite girl's name?

Anna

What is your favourite food?

Roast duck

What is your favourite music?

The cello

What is your favourite hobby?

Walking in the countryside

MEET THE ILLUSTRATOR– PHILIPPE DUPASQUIER

What is your favourite animal?

A tiger

What is your favourite boy's name?

Jonathan

What is your favourite girl's name?

Sophie

What is your favourite food?

Oysters

What is your favourite music?

Rock music

What is your favourite hobby?

Drawing

Contents

The Jungle House

Contents

The Snake Who Came To Stay

To everyone at
Miltonbank
Primary School

The Jungle House

Chapter 1
Mr Crocodile

When Dad told us Granny was going to come and live with us, my little brother Elmo said, "Is she going to sleep in the bath?"

"No, she'll need her own bedroom," said Dad. "We're going to have to look for a new house."

Granny couldn't live on her own any more because she kept getting into muddles. She had a black cat called Panther, and sometimes she put dry cat food instead of cat litter into the earth tray where he did his poos. Panther didn't mind – he just ate the food. But he did mind the day Granny put cat litter instead of cat food in his feeding bowl. Mum and Dad were

worried that Granny might start feeding herself the wrong things, or leave the oven on, or forget to turn the tap off.

We went to look at a lot of houses. The man who showed us round was called Mr Mills, but Elmo called him Mr Crocodile "because of his toothy smile".

Most of the houses we looked at had something wrong with them, but Mr Crocodile kept smiling and saying they were all "charming".

Then one day Mr Crocodile took us to see an empty house. The path up to the door had thick, tangly bushes growing over it. A pair of butterflies were fluttering about.

"This will be charming once the garden's all cut back," said Mr Crocodile, with one of his smiles, but Elmo and I liked it the way it was.

The front door had a lovely door knocker in the shape of a lion's head.

Inside, the house was all empty and echoey, and there were quite a lot of cobwebs. While Mum and Dad walked around slowly, talking with Mr Crocodile, Elmo and I raced about. We ran up the clattery stairs, and explored all the rooms and cupboards. One of the bedrooms had wallpaper with jungle trees and creepers on it and monkeys swinging about. There was a big cupboard in this room, the kind you can walk right into. Inside the cupboard was an extra large spider's web with a big fat spider sitting in the middle of it.

"Maybe it's a bird-eating spider," said Elmo.

When Mr Crocodile took Mum and Dad upstairs, Elmo and I raced up to them.

"We've got to buy this house!" I said.

"It's got butterflies and a lion and monkeys and a bird-eating spider," said Elmo. "It's a Jungle house!"

But Mum and Dad didn't look too sure, even when Elmo said he'd give them some of his pocket money to help pay for it. They said the extra bedroom was too small and dark for Granny.

"Mr Mills says the house next door is for sale too," said Mum. "We're going to have a look round that."

The lady who lived in the house next door just wasn't happy when she saw Elmo and me. She made us take our shoes off before she showed us round.

We followed the grown-ups round all the boring rooms. Most of them had flowery wallpaper. There was a flowery kind of smell too. I think it was from all the polish the fussy lady had been using on her tables and chairs.

After we left, Elmo said, "That was a horrible Flowerpot house! We *can't* move here! If we do, I'll run away."

But Dad just looked thoughtful, and said, "That sunny downstairs room would be just right for Granny."

We did move to the Flowerpot house. Mum, Dad and Granny liked it, and Panther seemed happy enough. But it didn't feel like home to Elmo and me.

Elmo hated the flowery wallpaper in his bedroom. He went round singing, "Roses are red, violets are blue, Flush the lot of them down the loo," for the first three days.

On the third day, Dad told him to get lost.

"All right," said Elmo, "I will." And the next thing we knew, he had gone.

Chapter 2
The Rusty Key

We looked all over the house and garden for Elmo. We even drove back to our old house in case he had run back there, but he hadn't. We started to get really worried then, and Mum rang the police.

While we were waiting for them to come I had an idea.

There was still no-one living in the Jungle house next door. I went out into our garden, which had short neat grass and no trees, and climbed over the wall. The grass in the Jungle garden was long and swishy. I stood still and listened. There was a rustle from inside one of the tangly bushes, and out jumped Panther. He trotted over to a tall thick tree and I followed him. The tree looked very old, and there was a big hole in the trunk, like a doorway. I peered inside. There, curled up and fast asleep, was Elmo.

After that we went to play in the Jungle garden every day. Sometimes Panther came with us. He chased butterflies and leaves. We pretended he was a real panther in a real jungle.

One day Panther was chasing some leaves under the hollow tree when I noticed something metal and rusty. It was an old key.

"Maybe it fits the back door of the Jungle house," I said.

We didn't really think it would, but when we tried it in the keyhole, it did.

The door opened with a creak, and we tiptoed inside.

The Jungle house looked just like the last time we'd seen it but now there were more cobwebs.

The spider in the cupboard of the monkey bedroom was looking even fatter than before. "That spider must have eaten a lot of birds," said Elmo.

We played jumping down the echoey stairs.

"I do wish we lived here," I said.

"Well, we can," said Elmo. "No-one else lives here, and we've got the key."

We came back the next day and the day after. We made a den in the big cupboard of the monkey bedroom. We took over some polish from our house and polished the lion door knocker till it shone. But we didn't clean anything else. We wanted the Jungle house to stay cobwebby and full of secrets.

One day we took Panther up to our den in the cupboard. We wanted him to meet the Bird-Eater. They were just saying hello when we heard voices and footsteps.

I picked up Panther. Elmo closed the door of the cupboard and we kept very quiet.

The footsteps came into the room. We heard Mr Crocodile's voice. He kept saying "charming". Then we heard another man's voice, a soft mumbly one. He kept saying, "Yes, yes …"

The footsteps came right up to the cupboard. Someone was turning the door handle! We pressed ourselves up against the wall behind the door. Mr Crocodile only opened the door a little bit. He said, "Another useful cupboard", and the other man said, "Perfect."

The cupboard door shut and the footsteps were going away when something awful happened. Panther wriggled and jumped out of my arms. He landed on the floor with a thud.

"Do we have a ghost?" the mumbly voice said. The next moment Mr Crocodile had opened the cupboard door again and found us.

Chapter 3
Mr Birdsnest

Mr Crocodile was very angry. For once he didn't give his crocodile smile. The other man, who had a white face and a long grey beard, said, "*Three* ghosts." We couldn't tell if he was angry or not.

Mr Crocodile took us back to the Flowerpot house. He made us give him the back-door key. Dad said we weren't to play next door again – not even in the garden.

"Why not?" Elmo said. "No-one lives there."

"The man who was looking round is probably going to buy it," said Dad. "He won't want you playing there."

"He must be a very greedy man if he wants the whole Jungle house all for himself," I said.

Elmo said the man probably had a lot of birds nesting in his beard and needed some rooms for them to fly around in. Mum told him not to be silly but I laughed. After that we called the man Mr Birdsnest.

We really missed playing in the Jungle garden. Mum and Dad had started to make a pond in our garden, but it wasn't finished yet. Elmo and I kept looking over the wall at the hollow tree next door. We kept muttering about mean old Mr Birdsnest.

A few weeks later a big removal van
drew up outside the Jungle house. Elmo and
I looked out of the window and watched the
men unload Mr Birdsnest's furniture. He
had a huge, long table with blankets
wrapped round the top of it. It was much
too big for one man.

"Greedy old Mr Birdsnest!" said Elmo.
"He must need an enormous table for his
enormous dinners."

"And look at all those boxes with blankets on top of them," I said. "What do you think is in them?"

"I bet it's the Crown Jewels," said Elmo.

Although we weren't allowed to go in the Jungle garden anymore, no-one could stop Panther playing there. The day after Mr Birdsnest moved in, Panther was sniffing around under the hollow tree when

the back door of the Jungle house opened
and a huge stripy cat ran out and pounced
on him. Panther raced back into our
garden.

"So Mr Birdsnest's got a tiger!" said Elmo.

Then out came Mr Birdsnest himself. He had a saw and he started sawing some thin branches off the hollow tree.

"Oh no," I said. "I bet he's going to cut it down."

"He's evil," said Elmo.

The next day we were in our garden when Elmo suddenly shouted, "Look!" and pointed to a window of the Jungle house. Someone was standing with their back to the window, and it looked like Granny.

"Mr Birdsnest has kidnapped her!" said Elmo.

We ran in to tell Mum and Dad. They were busy sticking dinosaur wallpaper up in Elmo's room. Mum just told us not to be so silly. She said that Granny was out posting a letter. The person at the window must be someone else.

But when we went back into the garden and looked up again, the person had turned round, and it *was* Granny. What's more, she was waving to us.

"She wants us to rescue her," I said.

Chapter 4
The Rescue

But how could we rescue Granny? We didn't have the key to the Jungle house any more.

"Perhaps the back door is open," I said.

We climbed over the wall and crept to the back door of the Jungle house. I turned the handle. The door creaked open.

"Let's leave it open in case we have to run for it," I said in a whisper.

We had often been in the jungle house before but this time it felt much scarier. I could feel my heart thumping as we tiptoed through the kitchen.

As soon as we opened the door from the kitchen into the hall we heard a noise – a kind of twittering and squawking.

"It's Mr Birdsnest's birds!" said Elmo.

It was true, the noise did sound like a lot of birds. It was coming from one of the downstairs rooms.

Elmo and I tiptoed past. We crept up the stairs.

When we got to the monkey bedroom we heard a clunking sound.

"What's that?" I whispered.

Just then there was another sound –
louder, this time, like a heavy ball falling.

What was Granny doing in there? And
was she locked in?

I turned the door handle. The door
opened.

There stood Granny, with a long stick in her hands. She was pointing it at a white ball which was sitting on the huge, long table we'd seen in the removal van.

And standing next to Granny, with another stick, was Mr Birdsnest!

"Ooh, you made me jump," said Granny.

"It's those ghosts again," said Mr Birdsnest.

We had planned to run if we saw him, but it didn't seem right. Mr Birdsnest was smiling, and so was Granny.

"I hope you don't mind me borrowing your grandmother," said Mr Birdsnest. "I found her on my doorstep."

Granny must have got into one of her muddles on the way back from posting her letter and gone to the wrong house.

"I asked her in for a cup of tea and a game of snooker," said Mr Birdsnest. "And now she's beating me."

Just then Granny got the black ball down a hole, which meant she had won. Good old Granny! I never even knew she could play snooker.

"Now," said Mr Birdsnest, "do you want to meet my friends?" He took us down to the room where we'd heard all the twittering and squawking.

When he opened the door we saw a sheet of wire netting right across the room from floor to ceiling. Behind the netting were lots and lots of brightly coloured birds. Some were flapping about and some were sitting on the branches Mr Birdsnest had cut off the hollow tree.

Elmo and I stared and stared. Then Elmo said, "Did you bring them all here in your beard?"

Mr Birdsnest laughed and said he'd brought them in cages covered with blankets.

"So it wasn't the Crown Jewels," said Elmo. Then he looked worried and said,

"Those birds had better watch out for the bird-eating spider!" Mr Birdsnest said it was all right. He had put the spider out in the garden where it was quite happy eating flies.

After that we were all friends, except for Tiger and Panther, and they seemed to enjoy being enemies.

Mr Birdsnest didn't cut the hollow tree down. Instead, he built a den up in the branches for me and Elmo. It had a door and a window, and a rope ladder to climb up to it.

So now we have our *own* Jungle house. It doesn't have monkey wallpaper of course, but when Mr Birdsnest found out how much we liked the lion door knocker he took it off his own front door and put it onto the tree house one: "In case your grandmother ever comes visiting."

The Snake
Who Came To Stay

Chapter 1
Holidays for Pets

"A snake?" said Mum. "A *snake*? No, you're not looking after a snake."

"Oh, go on, Mum," said Polly. "It's only for the holidays."

Polly knew Mum. Sometimes "No" could turn into, "I'll think about it."

"Doris is a very nice snake," said Polly. "I've met her. She's not poisonous or anything. Don't be mean, Mum!"

"Mean!" said Mum. "I like that! I've said *Yes* to two guinea pigs, a bird and a whole lot of goldfish. I just don't fancy having a snake in the house."

"But where else can Doris go?" asked Polly. "She can't go on holiday with Jack. And *we're* not going away. Oh, go on, Mum!"

"Well ..." said Mum, "I'll think about it. But I want you to take that notice down from the front gate."

The notice on the front gate said,

POLLY'S HOLIDAY HOME

HOLIDAYS FOR PETS

Going away this summer?

Why not give your pets
a holiday too?

Polly smiled as she took the notice down. She knew Mum. "I'll think about it" almost always meant "Yes."

Chapter 2
The Silent Snake

The first animals to arrive at Polly's Holiday Home were the two guinea pigs. They belonged to Polly's friend Katie and their names were Bill and Ben. Bill was thin and Ben was fat. They had their own house and garden. The house was a hutch, and the garden was a run – a box made of wire netting, which went on the grass.

Mum was quite pleased when she saw how fast Bill and Ben nibbled the grass. "If we move their run every day I won't need to get the lawn mower out all holidays," she said.

Bill and Ben needed extra food as well as the grass. When they were hungry they pushed their noses up to the wire netting and went "Oooeeek! Oooeeek! Oooeeek!" They made so much noise that you could hear them from the house.

A few days later, Mrs McNair from down the road brought her glossy black mynah bird round. "He likes to be in the kitchen so he can join in all the talk, don't you, Charlie?" she said.

"Ding dong," said Charlie. He sounded just like a door bell.

"I warn you, he copies *everything*, don't you, Charlie?" said Mrs McNair.

Charlie put his head on one side. Then, in a high warbly voice, he sang, "I dream of Jeannie with the light brown hair."

Mrs McNair laughed. "He's copying *me* now. That's my favourite song, isn't it, Charlie?"

"Bbrm bbrm," agreed Charlie. Now he sounded just like a motorbike.

The goldfish didn't have to come to the Holiday Home, because they were in a pond in the next-door garden. Polly just had to keep an eye on them and put more water in the pond if it didn't rain.

Doris the snake was the last animal to arrive. Jack brought her round in her tank. The tank had a little heater in it.

"But it's still best to keep her in the warmest room in the house," said Jack.

"That's the kitchen," said Mum with a sigh. "I won't have any space left to cook."

But she found a place for Doris on a worktop, in between Charlie's cage and the phone.

"Goodbye, Doris," said Jack.

Doris kept very still. She didn't even hiss.

"You see, Mum?" said Polly. "She'll be no trouble at all."

Chapter 3
The Copy Bird

The Holiday Home was a bit noisy for Mum, what with Bill and Ben oooeek-oooeeking and Charlie singing about Jeannie with the light brown hair all the time.

What's more, the phone kept ringing. More and more people wanted to know if Polly could take their pets. (Mum always said "No", and Polly didn't even try to turn it into "I'll think about it.")

But Doris the snake wasn't noisy at all. Sometimes she hissed – but only very softly.

"I told you she'd be good," said Polly.

One day Polly and Mum were having breakfast when the phone went yet again. Mum gave a sigh.

"I'll get it," said Polly. She picked up the phone and said hello, but there was no-one there.

Then they heard the ringing noise again. "Bbrring-bbrring, bbrring-bbrring."

It was Charlie.

Polly laughed, but Mum said, "I'm not having that!" and she moved Charlie's cage into the sitting room.

Later that day, Polly was outside feeding the guinea pigs when the postman arrived with two postcards for her. One of the cards was from Mrs McNair. It had a picture of a Spanish girl dancing. Polly took it into the sitting room and showed it to Charlie. He looked at the dancing girl and said, "Pretty boy!" The other card was from Jack. It had a picture of a vulture on it. On the back it said, "Show Doris the picture and tell her I'm missing her."

Polly went into the kitchen. She took the top off Doris's tank and put the card in. Doris gave a soft hiss.

At the same time Polly heard an extra loud, "Oooeeek! Oooeeek!" noise. "It's those guinea pigs. But they can't be hungry – I've just fed them. I hope nothing's wrong."

Polly ran back outside. Bill and Ben were in their wire run, eating their food.

"That's funny!" said Polly.

Then she heard the noise again. "Oooeeek! Oooeeek!" It was coming from inside the house. Polly laughed. She went back to the house, into the sitting room. There was Charlie, with his head on one side, going "Oooeeek! Oooeeek! OUEEEK!" just like Bill and Ben.

"You copy cat," she said.

"I dream of Jeannie with the light brown hair," Charlie replied.

All at once, Polly stopped laughing. She'd had an awful thought. She had been in such a rush to check that the guinea pigs were all right that she'd left the top off Doris's tank.

"But Doris wouldn't escape," she thought. "She's such a good, quiet, *still* kind of snake."

All the same, she ran back to the kitchen.

The tank was empty. Doris had gone.

Chapter 4
The Search

"She can't have gone far," thought Polly. She looked all round the room – in the sink, because she knew snakes like water, and under the radiator because they like to keep warm.

No Doris.

Polly lay on her tummy and tried to peer under the cooker. Just then Mum came in. "What *are* you doing?" she asked.

It was no use making something up.

"I'm looking for Doris," said Polly in a very small voice.

She knew what was coming next, and here it came.

"I *said* we shouldn't have a snake," said Mum. "I should never have said *Yes*."

She helped Polly look for Doris, but every now and then she said something like, "What if she turns up in my bed in the middle of the night?" which didn't help much.

It was bad enough having Mum cross, but it was Jack that Polly was really worried about. She knew he was already missing Doris – he'd said so on his postcard. How was he going to feel if she was gone forever?

Polly and Mum looked all over the whole house.

Mum had calmed down a bit. "Well, it's very odd," she said, "but I'm sure she'll turn up. Leave the lid off the tank and put some food in it."

But the days passed and Doris *didn't* turn up. Polly felt terrible. Jack was coming back from holiday next week. What was she going to say to him?

Then one day, Polly was watching TV when she thought she heard a faint hissing noise. She turned the TV off and listened.

Yes! There was the sound again. It was coming from near the window. Polly crept over. She pulled back one of the curtains and looked behind it. No Doris. And the hissing had stopped now.

Polly looked behind the other curtain. Nothing there. Then she heard the hiss again.

It was coming from Charlie's cage. He was hissing just like Doris. This time Polly didn't laugh.

Mrs McNair came back from her holiday in Spain. She had brought Polly a present – a Spanish doll that looked just like the dancing girl on the postcard.

"Has Charlie been a good boy?" she asked Polly.

"Er ... yes," said Polly and, "Oooeeek oooeeek!" said Charlie.

"I've got a new song for you, Charlie," said Mrs McNair. As she carried his cage outside she started to sing "You and your Spanish eyes" in her high warbly voice.

Suddenly she stopped singing and let out
a scream.

"What's the matter?" asked Polly.

"A snake!" screamed Mrs McNair.
"There's a snake on the doorstep!"

But it wasn't a snake. It was a snake
skin.

Chapter 5
Musical Pets

Jack had told Polly about how snakes grow a new skin and shed their old one, but Polly had never seen it happen. Now Doris's skin was lying on the doorstep. It was all thin and pale and papery, not a lovely bright green colour like Doris had been.

Mrs McNair got over her shock and took Charlie home. Polly was quite glad to see the back of him and to hear no more about Jeannie with the light brown hair.

Who cares about Jeannie with the light brown hair? she thought. *It's Doris with the bright green scales that I'm worried about.*

Where *was* Doris? She must be outside somewhere. Jack had told Polly that snakes didn't like the cold. They could die if it got too cold. The days had been quite warm and dry, but what about at night?

Polly looked all over the garden, but she couldn't find Doris.

"Have you seen her?" she asked Bill and Ben. And then she had a horrible thought. Snakes ate mice. What if they ate guinea pigs too?

Mum gave an extra loud sigh as she helped Polly to move Bill and Ben's hutch into the house. "I'm sick of playing musical pets," she said. "Why do we have to keep moving these animals around?" But Polly didn't want to take any risks. What if she had to tell Katie that her pets had been eaten by an escaped snake?

Jack was coming back from Blackpool the next day. Polly tried not to think about it as she squeezed through the gap in the hedge and went to have a look at the fish next door. It hadn't rained for a few days and the pond needed filling up.

Polly went into the next-door greenhouse to get the garden hose.

There were two hoses coiled up side by side. That was odd. Polly was sure there had only been one last time. One of the hoses was shorter and fatter than the other one, and it had some black markings on it. It was rather an odd hose. In fact, it wasn't a hose at all. It was Doris!

Chapter 6
Oooeeek! Oooeeek!

Jack came round the next day with another thank-you present for Polly. It was a book about tarantulas.

"Has Doris been good?" he asked.

"Er, yes ... very good," said Polly. She showed Jack the shed skin, but she didn't tell him everything – not yet.

The evening before Katie was due back, Mum gave Polly two carrots to feed to the guinea pigs. Thin Bill was standing at the front of the hutch going "Oooeeek, oooeeek, oooeeek!" But where was Ben? He was always so greedy, and he had got fatter than ever over the holidays.

Oh no! Don't say Ben's escaped now! thought Polly.

But that was impossible. The hutch door was shut. Then Polly heard a much softer "Oooeeek! Oooeeek!" noise. At least it couldn't be Charlie this time. He was safely back home with Mrs McNair.

The noise seemed to be coming from the back of the hutch. Very gently, Polly took out some of the hay. Yes, there was Ben. But the soft oooeeking wasn't coming from him.

Polly took out some more hay. There, cuddling up to Ben, were four baby guinea pigs.

So *that* was why Ben had looked so fat!

Chapter 7

Jeannie with the light brown hair

Katie came back from her holidays looking very brown.

"Have Bill and Ben been good?" she asked.

"Yes," said Polly. "But I've got something to show you."

Katie was very excited when she saw the baby guinea pigs. But she said, "Ben doesn't sound right for a mother guinea pig. I'll have to give her a new name. I know – Jen!"

Katie's thank-you present for Polly was a little box made of sea shells.

Polly liked all her presents – but the best one was still to come. When the baby guinea pigs were old enough to leave Jen, Katie asked if Polly would like to have one of them.

Polly asked Mum. "Oh, go on, Mum, *please*!" she said.

To her surprise, Mum said, "I'll think about it."

It was a little girl guinea pig. Polly called her Jeannie – because she had light brown hair.

Barrington Stoke would like to thank all its readers for commenting on the manuscript before publication and in particular:

Farida Ahmed
Ryan Allison
Robyn Bonnar
Abigail Braybrook
Lynne Brown
Jane Bulley
James Carmichael
Callum Cherry
Dylan Coolahan
Markus Coolahan
Callum Cunningham
David Dinwoodie
Leon Fargher
Katy Hadden
Gareth Hay
Hannah Janes
Darrell Jones

Lynn Linsell
Daniel McIntyre
Steven Moriarty
Alfie Newbiggin
V. O'Byrne
Liam Porteous
Bridget Rogers
Cicely Rotchell
Jemima Scott
Stephen Shore
Stacey Simpkins
Jake Snooks
Lorna Tordoff
Emma Watterson
William White
Natasha Wilson
Aham Zahoor

Become a Consultant!

Would you like to give us feedback on our titles before they are published? Contact us at the email address below – we'd love to hear from you!

info@barringtonstoke.co.uk
www.barringtonstoke.co.uk